SECRET SCHOOL SPY SQUAD
Mission 2: Germ Galore

Janelle McGuinness

Illustrations by FXNCOLOR STUDIO

This book is dedicated to the two little inspirations in my life
– Nina and Jessica.

Thank you to my family and friends for the support and encouragement, my husband and editor Damien, Tina, Giannina, Frank, Jacki, James and Emily.

Published by MCG Ventures Pty Ltd trading as Techiworx
BOX 22 / 9 Rohini Street
Turramurra NSW 2074
Australia
www.techiworx.com

For more information about these books and the author visit:
www.secretschoolspysquad.com

Cover design and illustrations by FXNCOLOR STUDIO (www.fxncolor.com)

All rights reserved. No part of this publication may be reproduced, stored, in a retrieval system, or transmitted in any way or by any means, electronic, mechanic, photocopying, recording or otherwise, without the prior written permission of MCG Ventures Pty Ltd.

ISBN: 978-0-9953822-3-7

Copyright ©2016 Janelle McGuinness

SECRET SCHOOL SPY SQUAD

Mission 2: Germ Galore

Written by Janelle McGuinness

Illustrations by FXNCOLOR STUDIO

I go to school like everybody else.
I learn to read, write and do maths like everybody else.
I have friends and we talk about, you know...stuff like everybody else.

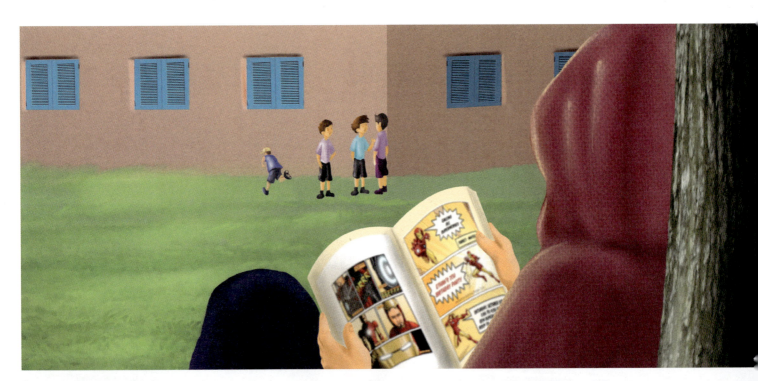

But I have a secret, a very important secret.
I'm a member of Secret School Spy Squad or Sx4 for short.

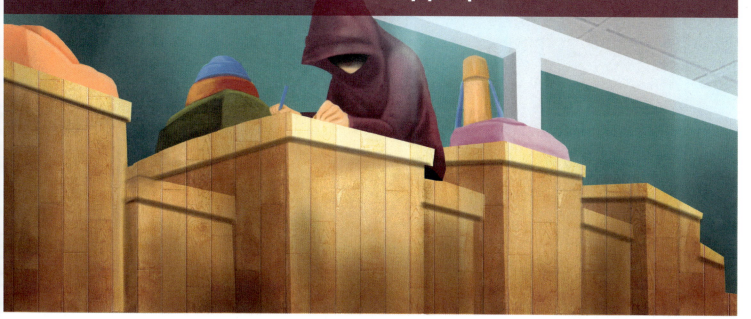

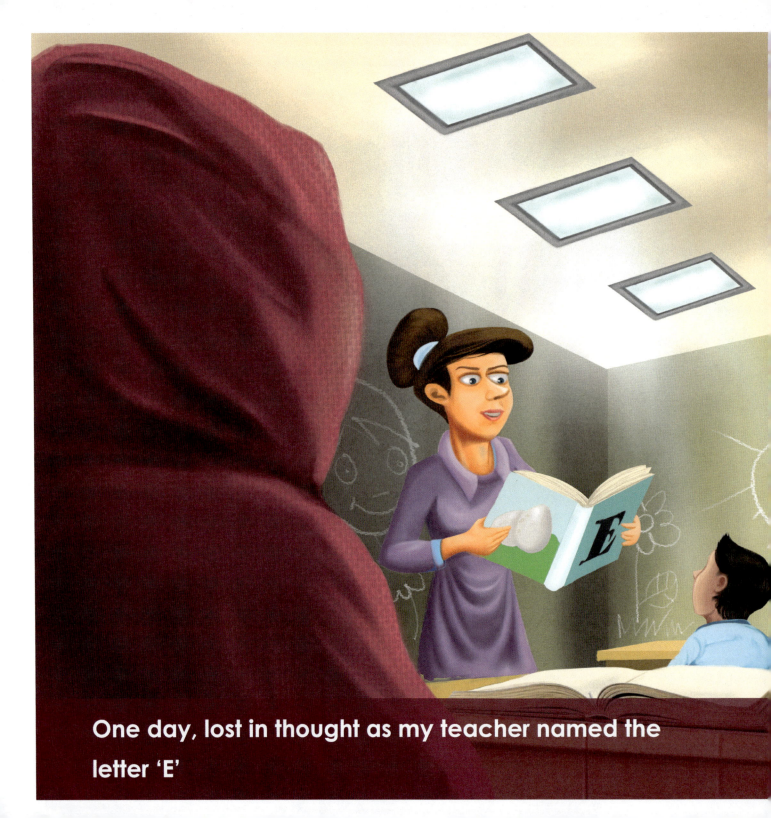

One day, lost in thought as my teacher named the letter 'E'

My watch began to shake, startled, I smiled with glee.

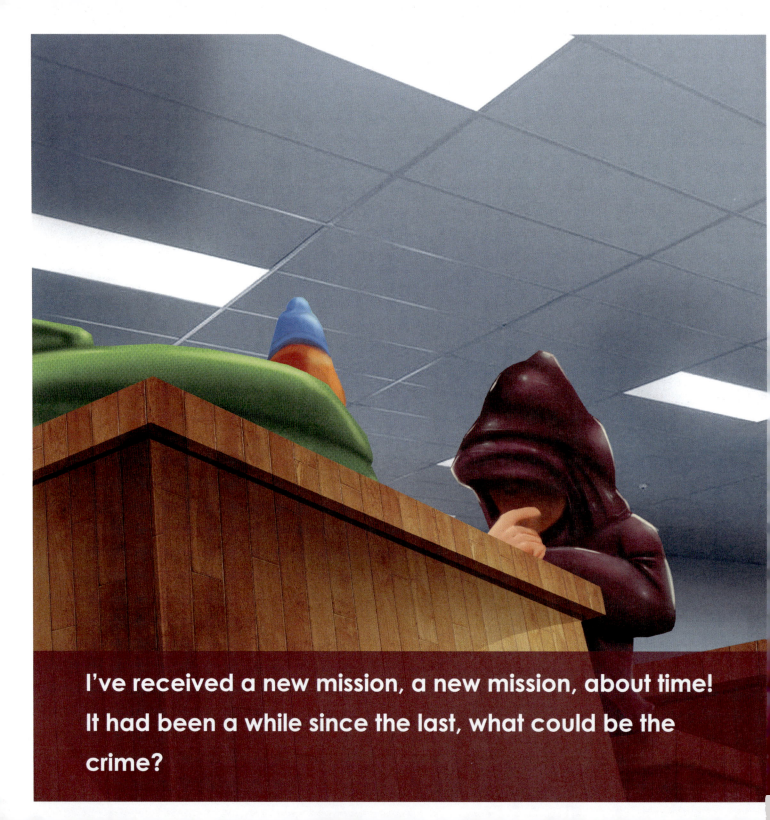

I've received a new mission, a new mission, about time! It had been a while since the last, what could be the crime?

I opened the secret spy pad in my bag which read...

SX4 AGENT N, STUDENTS ARE GETTING SICK AND MUST STAY IN BED. YOUR MISSION: FIND OUT WHAT'S CAUSING THIS. IT IS SO CRUEL. STOP THIS ILLNESS SO THE STUDENTS CAN RETURN TO SCHOOL

What could possibly be making the kids so sick?
Something toxic, or germs, whatever, I'd better be quick!

I asked the teacher what illness they were suffering from. She said an upset tummy, puking and the occasional D-bomb!

I'm no doctor but to me this sounds like something they ate. Doing some detective work, I must find what's sealing their fate.

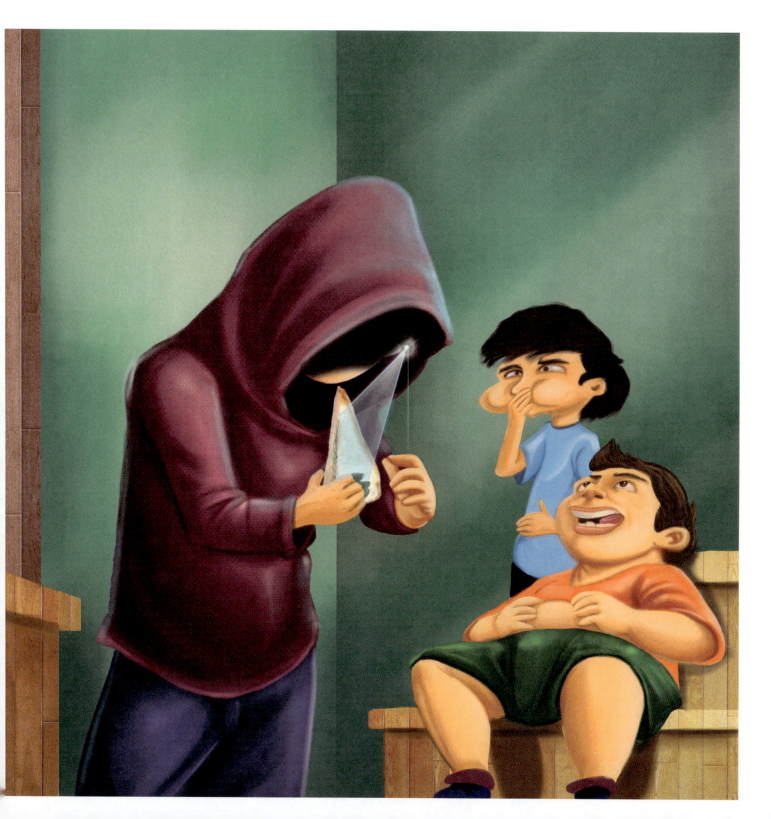

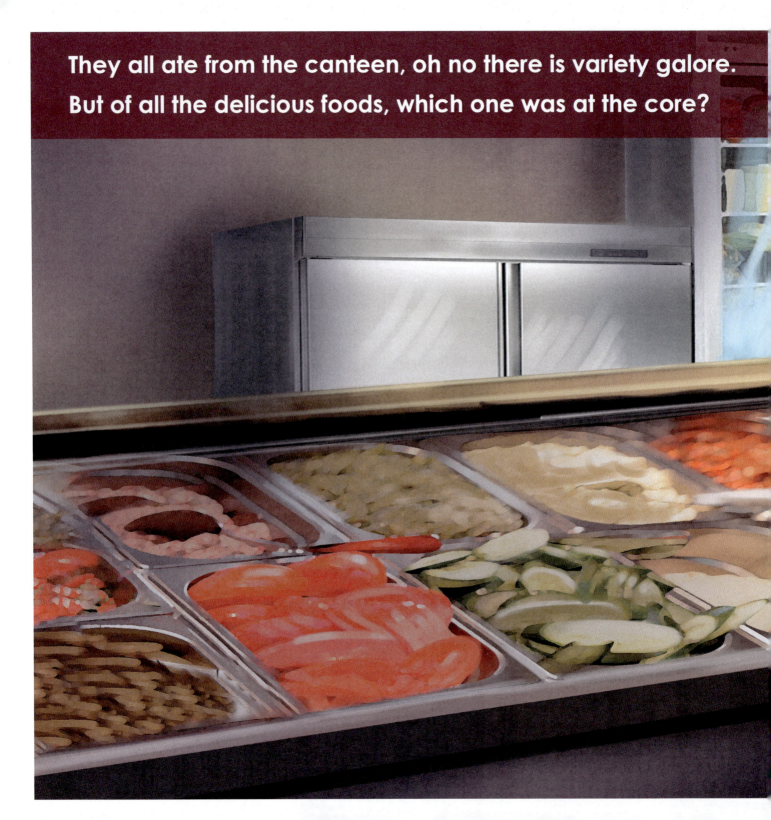

I ordered one of each item on the menu, pretending to be hungry.
With my spy microscope, I tested each to see which was dodgy.

The last item I tested definitely had something wrong.

WATER CONTENT
90%

14°

BACTERIA
FUNGUS
GERMS

YES

MAGNIFY
100%

INFECTED COMPLETELY

Packed full of germs, this'll make kids sick all day long.

So, which item was it? Of course one of the best.
The hot dog, nothing better with sauce to digest.

After further investigation and some serious interrogation. The hot dogs were delivered early with no refrigeration.

Somebody new was working in the canteen and arrived late.
They didn't realise this could happen from such a long wait.

Ah, another mission complete, my second badge received.
I'm getting the hang of this, I wouldn't have believed.

Secret School Spy Squad is tough going but a lot of fun. Especially when helping sick kids return to playing in the sun.

Thank you for purchasing this book!

I hope your young reader enjoyed it as much as I enjoyed writing it. If you liked the book, please take a couple of minutes to write an online review so that others can enjoy it too.

Some other books in the series:

Mission 1 – "Lost Lunchboxes"

Mission 3 – "Shrinking Students"

Mission 4 - "Hair-raising Hair

Want to be notified when new books become available?

Sign up at www.secretschoolspysquad.com or like the [Secret School Spy Squad](#) Facebook Page.

Who is Sx4 Agent N?

Are you wondering which school student is Sx4 Agent N? Visit our website www.secretschoolspysquad.com/whois.html to see information about each of the students and see if you can guess who.

I will give away a secret clue in each Sx4 book. Clue number one:

Sx4 Agent N has brown hair

Made in the USA
Middletown, DE
17 December 2019